PEANUTS

Happy Valentine's Day,
CHARLIE BROWN!

by Charles M. Schulz
adapted by Maggie Testa
illustrated by Scott Jeralds

Ready-to-Read

Simon Spotlight

New York   London   Toronto   Sydney   New Delhi

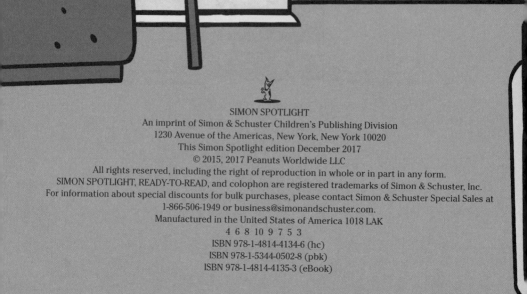

SIMON SPOTLIGHT
An imprint of Simon & Schuster Children's Publishing Division
1230 Avenue of the Americas, New York, New York 10020
This Simon Spotlight edition December 2017
© 2015, 2017 Peanuts Worldwide LLC
SIMON SPOTLIGHT, READY-TO-READ, and colophon are registered trademarks of Simon & Schuster, Inc.
For information about special discounts for bulk purchases, please contact Simon & Schuster Special Sales at
1-866-506-1949 or business@simonandschuster.com.
Manufactured in the United States of America 1018 LAK
4 6 8 10 9 7 5 3
ISBN 978-1-4814-4134-6 (hc)
ISBN 978-1-5344-0502-8 (pbk)
ISBN 978-1-4814-4135-3 (eBook)

Each February, Charlie Brown
makes valentines for all his
friends, plus a special one for the
Little Red-Haired Girl.
This year's valentine for her
is the nicest one yet.

And this year, Charlie Brown
is determined to deliver it!
It goes like this:

Your hair is red and full of curls.
You're sweeter than all other girls.
You make me want to laugh and cry.
I wish that I could be your guy.

As Charlie Brown is leaving his house
to deliver his special valentine,
he runs into his sister, Sally.
Sally is making a fortune-teller
valentine for her Sweet Babboo,
also known as Linus.

"No matter which fortune he chooses,
Linus will know how I feel,"
Sally says.
Every message tells Linus
that Sally wants him to be
her valentine!

Outside, Charlie Brown sees
Marcie and Peppermint Patty.
Peppermint Patty shows
Charlie Brown a chain of
paper dolls she has made.

"These dolls are like mistletoe,"
she explains and wiggles her eyebrows.
"If two people stand under them,
they have to hold hands."
Charlie Brown bolts away!

Soon he bumps into Pigpen.
Pigpen is busy picking up cereal,
nuts, raisins, and candy that
spilled onto the sidewalk.
"What is all this?"
asks Charlie Brown.

"I'm making my
Super Sweetheart Crunchy Munchies
for Snoopy's Valentine's Day party,"
answers Pigpen.
Snoopy is throwing a party?
This is news to Charlie Brown.

"My own dog is having a party
and didn't invite me," moans Charlie
Brown.
"Why would the Little Red-Haired
Girl want a valentine from me?"

Charlie Brown decides to
visit Lucy's booth.
He pays a nickel and explains
his problem.

"You need to speak up!"
Lucy advises.
"Tell Snoopy and the Little
Red-Haired Girl how you feel!"

Charlie Brown shudders
at the thought of speaking up.
"There's no sense being shy,"
Lucy tells him.
Then she shows Charlie Brown
the valentine she will give
to Schroeder at the party.

Charlie Brown feels better.
Lucy isn't afraid to express
her feelings.
He shouldn't be afraid either!

Charlie Brown marches right over
to Snoopy's doghouse.
"I've heard you're having a party,
and you invited everyone but me,"
he says.
"I'm the one who feeds you
and takes care of you."

Snoopy types something up
on his typewriter and hands it
to Charlie Brown.

Charlie Brown thinks it is an invitation.
Then he realizes it's just a list
of snacks Snoopy needs for his party.

Charlie Brown decides to go
straight to the Little Red-Haired
Girl's house.

But once he gets there,
he just can't bring himself
to even ring the doorbell.

So he stops at the store to buy snacks
and then goes to Snoopy's party.
When he arrives, the party is
in full swing.
Linus says, "Gee, Charlie Brown,
you just missed the
Little Red-Haired Girl."

Charlie Brown smacks his forehead.
"Good grief!" he cries.
He has the worst luck,
but at least someone has given him
a valentine.

Charlie Brown tears open
the envelope and finds a card
signed by all his friends.
It says . . .

"Happy Valentine's Day,
Charlie Brown!"